*L*OOKING AT *P*AINTINGS
Children

Three Studies of a Child Wearing a Cap, undated
Antoine Watteau, French (1684–1721)

LOOKING AT PAINTINGS

Children

Peggy Roalf

Series Editor
Jacques Lowe

Designer
Joseph Guglietti

Hyperion Books for Children
New York

A
JACQUES LOWE
VISUAL ARTS PROJECTS
BOOK

Printed in Italy

FIRST EDITION

1 3 5 7 9 10 8 6 4 2

Library of Congress Catalog Number: 92-52982

ISBN: 1-56282-309-4 (trade)/1-56282-308-6 (lib. bdg.)

Original design concept by Amy Hill

Contents

To Kelly, to love, to children

Introduction

*L*OOKING AT PAINTINGS is a series of books about understanding what great artists see when they paint. Children have been a favorite subject for painters since the time of the ancient Egyptians. One of the earliest surviving portraits of a child was created seventeen hundred years ago by an unknown Egyptian artist. He captured the luminous eyes and proud expression of a boy named Eutyches in a painting that was wrapped with the boy's mummy when he was buried.

Pieter Brueghel created a scene that expresses every child's dream: a world in which adults play no part. In *Children's Games*, a panoramic view of a village square completely taken over by young people, Brueghel depicted more than eighty different games, many of which are still played today.

Artists working for kings and nobles have painted portraits that symbolize their wealthy patrons' ambitions for their children. Agnolo Bronzino portrayed Giovanni de' Medici as an impish baby wearing luxurious silk clothes. Using costly pigments and paint made of real gold, he created a portrait that foretells Giovanni's future as a Roman Catholic cardinal.

When painters portray their own children, we see expressions of love in images that have deep personal meaning for the artists. Frank W. Benson captured the seemingly endless pleasure of his children's summer vacation in *Calm Morning*, a painting that radiates with light reflected from a peaceful harbor.

Great artists have expressed the joys and sorrows of young people from distant times and other cultures, often incorporating memories of their own childhood into the paintings. You can look at other children—your friends and classmates—and use your imagination to see like a painter.

PORTRAIT OF A BOY, second century A.D.
Unknown artist from Fayum, Egypt, encaustic on wood panel, 15" x 7½"

This portrait of a boy named Eutyches was created by an Egyptian artist who lived during a period of Roman rule. The artist adopted the contemporary style of Roman painting, using shadows and highlights to create an expressive portrait. Unlike ancient Egyptian tomb paintings—flat figures drawn in profile with sharp outlines—this portrait has a lifelike presence.

The painter used great skill and imagination to achieve dramatic effects with a limited range of colors. Before artificial pigments came into use, painters used colors made from natural materials. Yellow ochre, red, and brown pigments were made from clay; black was made from charred bones or soot from oil lamps; white was made by roasting chalk or oyster shells in an oven.

The fresh colors in this portrait were created through a technique called *encaustic*, which comes from a Greek word meaning "to burn in." The artist combined pigments with beeswax melted over a hot fire and produced creamy

opaque colors as well as thin transparent shades. When the painting was completed, the artist passed a hot metal pan over the surface to burn in the colors, permanently bonding them to the wooden panel on which he or she had painted.

The artist created skin tones by brushing transparent films of white over the evenly painted face. The boy's eyes are highlighted with opaque touches of luminous white that create a realistic warmth. With a few thinly painted shadows on the right side of the head, nose, and neck, he created a three-dimensional effect. The artist created interest in the white robe with a black stripe and a Greek inscription that spells the boy's name.

This moving portrait, which was wrapped with Eutyches's mummy and buried in his tomb, retains its original brilliance after nearly two thousand years.

9

EDWARD VI AS A CHILD, about 1538
Hans Holbein the Younger, German (1497?–1543), oil on panel, 22 ⅜" x 17 ⅜"

Hans Holbein the Younger was trained by his father, a prominent painter in Augsburg, Germany, and became an established artist in Basel, Switzerland, while still a teenager. In 1536, Holbein became the official painter of England's King Henry VIII on the recommendation of their mutual friend, the Dutch scholar Erasmus.

In this portrait of the two-year-old son of King Henry VIII and the third of his eight wives, Jane Seymour, Holbein captured the essence of royal power. Holbein shaped a powerful composition through the child's dynamic pose: grasping a golden rattle in one tiny hand, Edward raises the other in a kingly gesture and looks at the viewer with unwavering eyes. Because there are no everyday objects in the painting to compare in size with the figure, Edward seems larger than life.

Using paints made of real gold and costly red pigment, Holbein captured the luxurious textures of soft velvet and stiff embroidered silks. Holbein used the technique of foreshortening, decreasing the distance between the child's right hand and shoulder to create the appearance of correct proportion when viewed straight on. With brilliant white paint on the cuffs, blouse, and hat, he separated the figure from the dark background. Light spills into the scene from the right. This effect, along with soft shading and highlights, gives the figure its solid form.

Holbein's commanding portraits of England's royal family made him the favorite painter of King Henry VIII. Holbein spent the rest of his life in England and developed a style of court portraiture that endured for the next hundred years.

Ambrosius Holbein, Hans Holbein the Younger's brother, captured the pensive mood of this boy in a silver point drawing. With a pointed silver rod, he made pale gray lines that turned black as the silver particles from the rod tarnished.

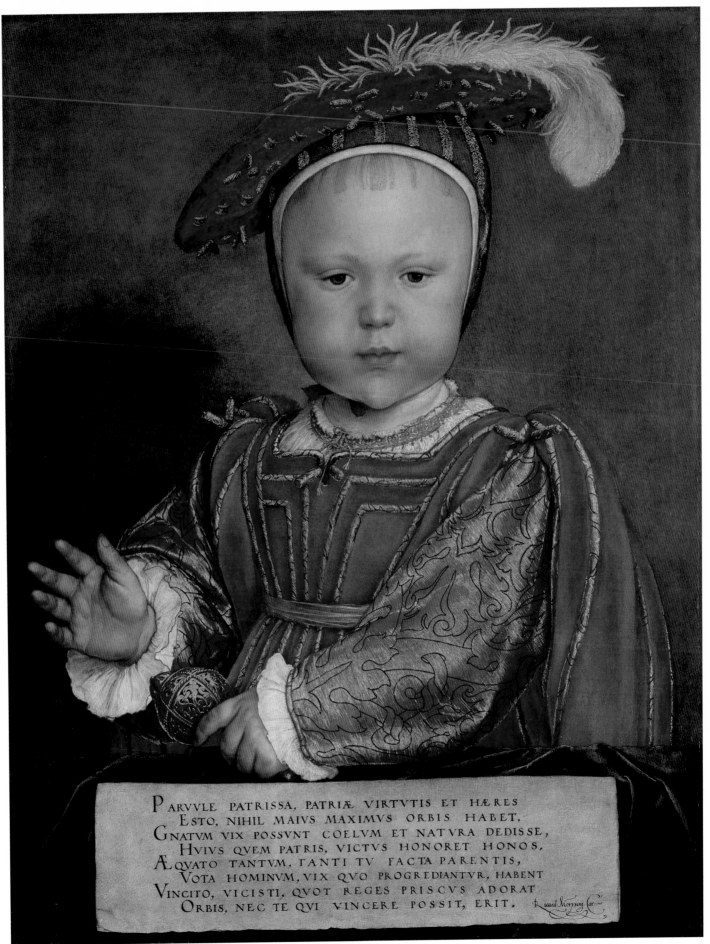

PARVVLE PATRISSA, PATRIÆ VIRTVTIS ET HÆRES
  ESTO, NIHIL MAIVS MAXIMVS ORBIS HABET.
GNATVM VIX POSSVNT COELVM ET NATVRA DEDISSE,
  HVIVS QVEM PATRIS, VICTVS HONORET HONOS.
ÆQVATO TANTVM, TANTI TV FACTA PARENTIS,
  VOTA HOMINVM, VIX QVO PROGREDIANTVR, HABENT
VINCITO, VICISTI, QVOT REGES PRISCVS ADORAT
  ORBIS, NEC TE QVI VINCERE POSSIT, ERIT.   Ricard: Morysyn Car=

GIOVANNI DE' MEDICI AT EIGHTEEN MONTHS, 1545

Agnolo Bronzino (born Agnolo di Cosimo), Italian (1503–72), tempera on panel, 22⅞" x 19"

*A*gnolo Bronzino and his patron, Cosimo de' Medici, each gained prestige and power through accidental opportunities. When his distant relative Alessandro was murdered in 1537, Cosimo was elected duke of Florence, Italy. Soon after, he noticed Bronzino's talent when the young apprentice was working on a mural at the Medici palace. Cosimo then selected Bronzino as his official painter.

Bronzino embellished this portrait with emblems that foretell Giovanni de' Medici's future. As the second son of Cosimo, Giovanni would become a clergyman, whereas his older brother, Francesco, would inherit their father's title. Giovanni's wine-colored tunic symbolizes the red robes worn by cardinals of the Catholic church. The goldfinch, a traditional symbol of the infant Christ, implies the divinity of Giovanni's birth.

Through the use of contrasting elements, Bronzino created a majestic portrait that expresses the Medici's status and ambition. The baby's amused expression seems more adult than childlike. His tousled hair and chubby hands contrast with the stiff pose and elaborate costume. Bronzino, famous for the icy brilliance of his painting technique, created warm, lifelike skin tones by applying a transparent rosy glaze to the face and hands. The use of contrast extends to the cold green background that emphasizes the warm colors in the baby's face and clothing.

Bronzino, who referred to this child as an angel, affectionately captured the freshness of an infant who would become a cardinal at the young age of seventeen.

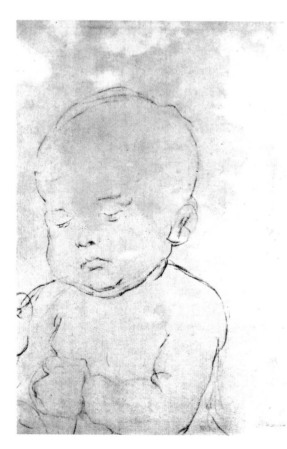

With a few fluidly drawn lines of chalk on textured paper, Andrea del Verrocchio (1435–88) captured a sleepy infant's soft features.

CHILDREN'S GAMES, 1560

Pieter Brueghel, Flemish (1525/30–69), oil on oak panel, 46 ½" x 63 ⅜"

Pieter Brueghel often detailed the joys and sorrows of Flemish peasantry. For sixteenth-century farmers, life consisted of backbreaking labor, high taxes, and constant war. Young people toiled as hard as their parents. When work came to a halt for religious holidays, the children played as hard as they worked.

In this painting, Brueghel chose a high viewpoint looking down on a village completely taken over by children. He created a visual encyclopedia of games: there are more than eighty different activities in this scene, from playing marbles and rolling hoops in the foreground to jousting on piggyback in the middle to blindman's buff in the background.

Brueghel brought order to this busy scene through the placement of objects and buildings and the arrangement of games in distinct groups. A long table slants in from the right; the diagonal side of a barn on the left points to the center of the scene where a group of children imitate adults in a mock wedding procession. To keep our gaze from wandering out of the picture, Brueghel walled off the background with a tall building that prompts us to notice two acrobatic boys swinging on a hitching post.

Through the careful balance of bright and soft colors, Brueghel defined the figures, which stand out clearly from the golden earth. The red paint that he used for many of the costumes leads our eyes through the games to the distant landscape where they continue.

Brueghel depicted these young people with old faces enjoying a day of stolen pleasure to express his sympathy for peasant children forced to shoulder adult responsibilities.

Brueghel used the contrast of light and dark colors to separate the figures in this tug of war game.

BOY IN A CORAL NECKLACE, about 1619
Peter Paul Rubens, Flemish (1577–1640), black and red chalk heightened with white chalk on paper, 9 15/16" x 7 15/16"

Like many of his successful contemporaries, Peter Paul Rubens had royal patrons. Archduke Albert and Archduchess Isabella, rulers of the Low Countries (present-day Belgium, Luxembourg, and the Netherlands), commissioned imposing portraits to impress visiting foreign nobles. There was such a demand for his paintings that Rubens trained assistants to help with the preparatory work. He first made drawings, which the helpers transferred onto canvas. Following their master's precise instructions, the assistants applied the initial layers of paint. Later, Rubens applied his personal touch: details and transparent layers of color, called glazes, that brought the paintings to life.

To relax from the hectic pace of the workshop and his demanding patrons, Rubens often made drawings, such as this one of his son. Using crayons harder than charcoal but softer than wax, Rubens captured the softness of his son Nicolas's face, the crystalline clarity of his eyes, and the feathery wisps of his hair. Rubens formed gray shadows with fine, overlapping black lines called *cross-hatching.* He then added broad strokes of red chalk that suggest the child's healthy coloring. Using white chalk, he created highlights that focus our attention on the beauty of his son's features and guide our eyes from the touches of white on the necklace to the boy's lips, nose, and eyelids.

Rubens made many paintings and drawings of his children for his own enjoyment. These images, created by his hand alone, convey the love and contentment Rubens must have felt at home.

Through the contrast of crosshatch shading and areas of blank paper, Rubens created the impression of light in the drawing of his son, Peter Paul. The artist made this study in preparation for the painting, Rubens, His Wife Hélèna Fourment, and Their Son Peter Paul.

16

P P Rubens

GEORGE AND FRANCIS VILLIERS, 1635
Anthony Van Dyck, Flemish (1599–1641), oil on canvas, 54" x 50¼"

*A*nthony Van Dyck, the most famous pupil of Peter Paul Rubens, moved from Belgium to England in 1632. As the official painter of King Charles I, Van Dyck created portraits of the royal household, which included George and Francis Villiers. The two boys were raised with Charles's children after the death of their father, who had been the king's closest friend and England's prime minister.

Using colored chalk, Raphael (1483–1520) drew parallel curved lines that follow the contours of this boy's face to create shadows that make this drawing appear three-dimensional.

Van Dyck created a psychological as well as a realistic portrait that was unusual for his time. Van Dyck captured the arrogant attitude of George Villiers, from his scornful expression to his defiant pose. The younger boy, Francis, looks nervously at his brother and fidgets with his cape.

By placing the two figures against a dark background, Van Dyck spotlights the extraordinary painting technique with which he captured the shimmer, the movement—almost the rustling sound—of the boys' silk robes. This technique is called "fat over lean." Van Dyck would begin with dark-toned colors thinned with turpentine. After the thin, or lean, layer was dry, he applied brighter tones. These he thickened, or fattened, with oil, blending the colors on the canvas while the paint was wet. Through this technique, Van Dyck ensured that the thicker layers of color would not crack as the paint dried. Today this portrait glows with the same clarity and brilliance that it originally had over 350 years ago.

In his lifetime, Van Dyck created more than five hundred portraits. He introduced an aristocratic painting style to a country that had produced brilliant writers, such as William Shakespeare, but few talented painters.

PORTRAIT OF THE INFANTA MARGARITA, undated
Diego Rodríguez de Silva Velázquez, Spanish (1599–1660), oil on canvas,
27½" x 23"

King Philip IV of Spain struggled to keep his country from collapsing under the pressure of war with France. To temporarily end the conflict between the two nations, Philip arranged the marriage of his daughter, Marie-Thérèse, to Louis XIV of France. As the two had never met and travel was dangerous and difficult, Philip used portraits created by Diego Velázquez to proclaim her beauty.

Velázquez also painted a series of portraits of Margarita, the youngest and prettiest Spanish princess, to promote her engagement to Leopold I of Austria. Every few years, Philip sent a new painting of Margarita to Leopold's parents to impress them with her health and beauty as she grew up.

A limited selection of paint colors was available to seventeenth-century European painters. In Velázquez's hands not only his subjects but also the paint itself seem alive. Velázquez first painted Margarita's gown in a bluish gray tone. Over this he applied a thin layer of white that allows the blue-gray tone to show through, creating the effect of folds in the fabric. The inky shadows, a signature detail in Velázquez's work, make the few colors—red, black, and white—seem incandescent. Rather than creating realistic details, Velázquez captured the light flickering across satin rosettes and jewelry with almost abstract dashes of thick white paint. Using the same bold brushwork, Velázquez painted Margarita's hair in a blur of color that comes into focus with a few keenly observed highlights.

Velázquez's fondness for the little princess is apparent in this official portrait and in his greatest masterpiece, *The Maids of Honor*, which he created in about 1656 for King Philip's personal enjoyment.

DON MANUEL OSORIO MANRIQUE DE ZUÑIGA, about 1787–88
Francisco de Goya y Lucientes, Spanish (1746–1828), oil on canvas, 50" x 40"

Francisco de Goya y Lucientes's passionate desire for success propelled him along a difficult journey. Born in the poor, isolated village of Fuendetodos, Spain, Goya learned his craft as an apprentice artist in the provincial city of Zaragoza. He moved to Madrid in 1763, where he struggled to make ends meet by working as an assistant. Teaching at the Royal Academy, Goya made contact with noble families who commissioned portraits and murals. After several rejections, Goya was finally accepted as a painter to King Charles III of Spain in 1789.

In this portrait of the Count of Altamira's son, we see Goya's masterly command of contrasting colors, textures, and light. Goya painted Don Manuel's fashionable red suit in broad strokes almost uninterrupted by shadows or details. In contrast, the white lace collar and satin sash glow with light, transparency, and delicately painted details. Goya emphasized the boy's rosy skin tone through the contrasting gray-green background.

Goya displays his gift for telling a powerful story through the use of symbols that were readily understood in his time. Standing alone in an empty room, the boy is surrounded by pets that represent both good and evil. The three menacing cats are poised to pounce on the magpie, a Christian symbol of goodness. The caged birds represent childhood.

Goya created an air of mystery through the strong shadow on the right that suggests an open door spilling light onto the boy. He leaves the viewer with an unanswered question: what does the child see on the other side of the door?

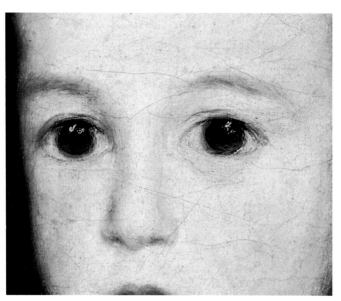

A detail of Don Manuel de Zúñiga's face shows that Goya defined the child's features with tones of pink and the same gray-green color of the background.

EL S D MANVEL OSORIO MANRRIQVE DE ZV

BABY IN RED HIGH CHAIR, about 1800–25
Unknown American artist, oil on canvas, 22" x 15¼"

*a*merican folk art evolved as a tradition far removed from elegant drawing rooms in New England and great plantations in the South. Whereas artists who had studied in Europe created refined portraits and landscape paintings that expressed the status of their wealthy clients, a group of largely unknown artisans mostly in rural communities created paintings for a different audience. These painters were often highly trained in the craft of sign painting and decorating but unschooled in classical art traditions. Through observation and imagination they created simple, but often expressive, paintings to record important events in the lives of ordinary people.

A Pennsylvania artist captured the angelic expression of a sleeping infant in this loving portrait. With delicate touches of umber paint, the artist defined the baby's sweet features and downy cap of hair. The painter emphasized the softness of the baby, its clothing, and its blanket through the contrast between pale tones of white, ivory, and peach and the stark black background.

Using the technique of foreshortening, the artist decreased the distance between the feet and knees to create a sense of depth. The baby's little feet project toward the viewer and actually seem to press against the surface of the painting. The chair, however, is painted flatly, almost mechanically. The viewer does not sense that the chair is three-dimensional, like the figure.

Although this painting was created almost two hundred years ago, it looks contemporary. The figure, large in proportion to the size of the canvas, engages us with its simplicity and clear expression.

In 1837, American folk artist Isaac Sheffield painted this portrait of James Francis Smith, a sea captain's son, to celebrate the boy's safe return from a whaling expedition to the Antarctic. In the background, Sheffield included the ship on which Smith had traveled.

THE FIFER, 1866
Edouard Manet, French (1832–83), oil on canvas, 63" x 38⅛"

Today it is difficult to understand why Edouard Manet's paintings outraged art critics of his time. Even this portrait of a young fifer provoked harsh comments. One critic wrote that it looked flat, like a playing card illustration. Art experts of the nineteenth century preferred paintings that glorified human activity through the choice of historical themes or through an elegant, polished painting technique. Manet, however, often depicted ordinary people, such as this young cadet. He simplified details to create a strong impact, but for many of his contemporaries this gave the impression of an unfinished work.

The clarity of this composition reveals Manet's genius. He posed the fifer straight on, creating the largest possible area for the costume, which he painted in blocks of strong colors: red, black, and white. Areas of scarlet, broken by soft shading, form the trousers. Two curving bands of black outline the figure and give it form, and a row of golden buttons and a white sash enliven the solid black jacket.

Manet composed the upper part of the boy's figure in a series of jaunty angles that animate the still pose: the black fife is perpendicular to the golden fife; the angles formed by the boy's elbows are echoed by his fingers and the tricolor decoration on his hat.

Manet painted a background devoid of details but alive with the effect of light. By adding red to the gray, which is a mixture of black and white, he created a luminous tone that echoes the colors in the figure. Manet added darker shades of gray at the top and bottom of the canvas, focusing our attention on the color scheme. Manet created a picture that is not only a wonderful portrait but also a bold demonstration of his talent as a painter.

THE DAUGHTERS OF EDWARD D. BOIT, 1882
John Singer Sargent, American (1856–1925), oil on canvas, 87" x 87"

John Singer Sargent's parents believed that the great cultural centers of Europe would provide the best education for their children. Sargent's father gave up a medical practice in Philadelphia and moved the family to Florence, Italy, where the artist was born in 1856. After completing his studies in Paris, Sargent created this group portrait of the daughters of his friend Edward Boit, an American artist who also lived in the French capital.

Sargent was fascinated by photography, which had recently become widely practiced through the introduction of small hand-held cameras. In a painting that is more than seven feet high, Sargent echoed the qualities of a snapshot. Even the square shape, unusual for a painting, is the same as many photographs of the time. His young subjects look with questioning eyes at the viewer, as though interrupted during an important activity. Sargent painted the two figures in the foreground as well as the opulent carpet with clearly defined details. He blurred the distant figures in a way that suggests the out-of-focus background often seen in photographs.

Sargent created a space filled with objects that are enormous compared to the children. He posed the four girls in a vast, empty hall whose dark walls disappear into inky shadows. Their white pinafores lead our eyes from the spacious foreground to a glowing window far off in the distance. The smallest child sits on a large, wedge-shaped carpet that points toward a vase that towers over her older sisters. With a vertical slice of red and another gigantic vase, Sargent defined the right side of the canvas.

Through the intriguing composition and the children's somber expressions, Sargent evokes a serious mood. He shows his understanding that childhood can be a time of curiosity and endless waiting.

In this detail, we can see that Sargent painted broad, almost abstract strokes of white on the girl's dress that look realistic when seen from a distance.

CHILDREN PLAYING ON THE BEACH, 1884
Mary Cassatt, American (1844–1926), oil on canvas, 38⅜" x 29¼"

Mary Cassatt decided to become a professional artist during a family visit to Europe when she was seven years old; she was inspired by the great paintings she saw in art museums and galleries. After completing four years of training at the Pennsylvania Academy of Fine Arts, Cassatt convinced her family to support her studies in Paris, where she moved when she was twenty-one. Three years later, Cassatt received public recognition with the exhibition of her work at the 1868 Paris Salon, which was sponsored by the French Academy.

Cassatt created a holiday mood in *Children Playing on the Beach*, a painting alive with color and light. Although this picture looks spontaneous, Cassatt carefully organized the composition by making detailed drawings. Repeated angles, shapes, and colors focus our attention on two toddlers absorbed in play. Their arms and legs and a toy shovel—positioned at angles—slant into the picture. The dresses, silvery pails, and poses of the children are nearly identical. A close-up view from above sets the two figures off from the large expanse of sand and water in the background.

Cassatt captured the bright but shadowless quality of sunlight filtered through a hazy sky. With strong, or high-key, colors, she depicted the children's sunburned faces and arms. Highlights of thick white paint sparkle like reflected light on the pinafores. The toned down, or low-key, grays and blues in the distant ocean and sky make the figures seem brighter by contrast.

Edgar Degas made this drawing of Giovanna Bellelli in preparation for a large group portrait of her family. He formed the shadows through the technique of cross-hatching, using black chalk on pink paper.

In 1873, Mary Cassatt's talent and independent spirit came to the attention of the great French artist Edgar Degas (1834–1917). Degas became a longtime friend and mentor to the gifted American painter.

TO CELEBRATE THE BABY (Child with Puppet), 1903
Henri Rousseau, French (1844–1910), oil on canvas, 39⅜" x 31⅞"

Henri Rousseau worked as an inspector for the customs department in Paris and was a dedicated "Sunday painter." When he retired in 1893 to become a full-time artist, Rousseau endured grinding poverty in order to live a life of Sundays. Being a painter was the life Rousseau had dreamed of, and his sense of wonder and joy comes through in his work.

Like American folk artists, Rousseau was self-trained. But unlike those mostly rural artists who were isolated from mainstream academic art, Rousseau studied paintings in the Louvre museum and in the art galleries of Paris. Through observation and dedication to refining his technique, Rousseau mastered a painting style that expressed his artistic vision. There is nothing primitive or naive about this painting of a child, for it demonstrates Rousseau's command of color, contrast, and composition.

In this amusing family portrait, Rousseau depicts a baby that appears to be older and wiser than the adults.

Rousseau created a strong composition by exaggerating the size of the child compared to the scale of the landscape. He contrasted the baby's pale complexion, white gown, and chubby form with a brightly painted marionette constructed of hard-edged shapes and sharp angles. Rousseau united these contrasting colors and shapes with circular and curved elements: a ring of posies, which echoes the colors in the bouquet and in the puppet; the arch-shaped branches of the tree, whose lacy leaves mimic the child's wispy tendrils of hair.

Rousseau's paintings were admired in his lifetime by the public and by other artists, including Pablo Picasso (1881–1973). But Rousseau was a poor businessman. He often sold his work for the cost of a cheap meal and gave music lessons to make ends meet.

CALM MORNING, 1904
Frank W. Benson, American (1862–1951), oil on canvas, 44" x 36"

Every summer Frank W. Benson moved with his family to an island farmhouse off the coast of Maine. Benson felt renewed by the unspoiled natural beauty of the North Atlantic coast and created many portraits of his children in these idyllic surroundings.

In *Calm Morning*, Benson captured the bliss of a holiday in a place where the sun always shines. Benson created a composition based on classical standards. He posed three of his children—George, Elisabeth, and Sylvia—in a distinctly triangular arrangement that anchors the design. Deep shadows below the rowboat further strengthen the composition. The diagonal placement of the boat along with a high point of view lead the viewer into the scene. Through the use of traditional *perspective*, he created an illusion of depth and space by painting the fleet of sailboats progressively smaller as they recede toward the horizon.

Benson transformed his observations of hazy sunlight into golden highlights and pale blue shadows. He captured the reflected light inside the boat with curving strokes of yellow and blue that also depict the shape of the hull. Using the same colors, he defined soft shadows on the children's white clothes. A few swirls of paint in deeper shades of yellow and blue capture the light shining against the boat's transom. The pink in Sylvia's dress forms a soft contrast with the array of yellow and blue hues in the foreground.

Like Winslow Homer (1836–1910), Benson was fascinated by the changing light and colors of coastal Maine. Whereas Homer often depicted the frightening power of ocean storms, Benson captured the peaceful beauty of a calm harbor.

For this portrait of Alice Trask, Thomas Anschutz (1851–1912) used pastels—soft sticks of colored chalk—to depict the variety of textures in her fur coat, silk ribbon, and angora hat.

PORTRAIT OF CLAUDE RENOIR, CALLED COCO, about 1906
Pierre-Auguste Renoir, French (1841–1919), oil on canvas laid on board, 6½" x 5"

Pierre-Auguste Renoir expressed his enjoyment of life in luminous paintings of idyllic landscapes, happy children, and beautiful women. This portrait of his youngest son, Claude, nicknamed Coco, declares the fatherly love and pride Renoir felt for the child who was born when the painter was fifty-nine years old. He captured Coco's energy in a portrait that seems to radiate with light and energy.

In this full-length portrait of Robert Nunès, Renoir emphasized line through the angular pose, the boy's clearly outlined features, and the striped trimming on the suit.

In the 1880s, Renoir had experienced a crisis in his work: he believed that he was not progressing as a painter. In his search for new means of expression, he developed an oil painting technique very much like watercolor methods. In this portrait, which is a quickly made study for a large painting, we can see how Renoir worked. First, he sketched the composition directly onto canvas, using a brush and red-brown paint thinly diluted with turpentine. When this layer was dry, he created highlights on Coco's face and hair with light colors, also thinned with turpentine. The first layer of red-brown paint, which also covers the background, glows through the highlights to create a soft, three-dimensional effect we can almost touch and feel. Clean lavender shadows complement the golden highlights on Coco's hair, face, and shirt. Because Renoir blended colors directly on the canvas like a watercolorist, rather than mixing them on the palette, he maintained the freshness and clarity of the hues.

There is an effortless quality in this portrait that conceals Renoir's self-imposed demands to evolve as a painter. Even when he was old and afflicted with arthritis, Renoir continued to refine his technique—working with brushes taped onto his crippled hands—and to create paintings illuminated by his passion for life.

GIRL WITH BRAIDS, 1918
Amedeo Modigliani, Italian (1884–1920), oil on canvas, 23⅝" x 17⅞"

Like other young painters from all over the world, Amedeo Modigliani was attracted to the Paris art world. Fascinated by the primitive art he had seen in a natural history museum, Modigliani put aside painting and began to carve sculpture. He created elongated heads in simplified forms that suggest Stone Age idols. Because of poor health, which worsened due to alcohol and drug abuse, Modigliani could not sustain the physical demands of sculpting. He returned to painting and created haunting portraits that evoke the mystical quality of his sculpture.

In this painting, Modigliani simplified the young girl's figure, eliminating distracting details in the way a sculptor chips away unnecessary material from a block of stone. Precisely drawn lines that vary in thickness give the figure a sense of mass. As in his sculpture, Modigliani emphasized geometric shapes—the oval head and eyes, the triangular nose, and the rectanglular forms in the background. Through vertical shapes and the vertical format of the canvas Modigliani accentuated the elongated figure.

Modigliani reinforced the clarity of lines and shapes by selecting contrasting colors: red and green, black and white. A range of warm red tones—in the face, the shirt, and the background—focuses our attention on the girl's green eyes. To convey a sense of depth, Modigliani applied a translucent area of white behind the figure.

Two years after he created this portrait, Modigliani received his first public acclaim through an exhibition held in London. He died the following year, his life cut short by self-destructive habits.

Pierre Bonnard (1867–1947) exaggerated the awkward movement of a little girl burdened by a heavy basket by depicting her figure as a silhouette.

39

NELLIE WITH TOY, 1925
Otto Dix, German (1891–1969), oil and tempera on wood, 21¼" x 15½"

Otto Dix was inspired by fifteenth-century Renaissance art. In *Nellie with Toy*, we can see that Dix created a personal interpretation of the Holbein portrait that appears on page 10.

Dix portrays his daughter as a princess and shows us the emotions of a young child struggling to assert her will. In place of a tiara, she wears an outrageous pink bow. Before her are the symbols of royal power: a tower of wooden rings is her scepter; a shocking pink ball, her orb. She confronts the viewer, tearfully defying any challenge to her authority.

Dix created the brilliant colors and enamellike finish in *tempera*, a painstaking technique originally perfected during the Renaissance. In tempera, every aspect of the composition must first be studied in a drawing called a *cartoon*, which becomes the painter's working plan. Pure pigments are blended in advance; each hue is then combined with an equal amount of fresh egg yolk, which tempers, or sets, the pigment in a fluid state.

After transferring the cartoon onto the panel, Dix mixed the tempera with water to allow the paint to flow from the brush. He first shaped the large areas—Nellie's face, her clothes, the background—in thinly painted translucent layers. He "hatched" in shading, highlights, and details with distinct brushstrokes that allow the colors beneath to glow through.

Using a traditional painting technique, Dix created a modern commentary on the extremes of childhood emotions based on a Renaissance masterpiece.

L'IL SIS, 1944
William H. Johnson, American (1901–70), oil on canvas, 26" x 21¼"

William H. Johnson was an African-American painter who received his formal training at the New York Academy of Design. Early in his career, he worked in a style inspired by the great modern European painters such as Vincent van Gogh (1853–90). After a 1932 visit to Africa, where he explored his ancestral legacy, Johnson developed what he called a "primitive" style of painting to express his feelings about the black experience. He then turned to memories of his own childhood in the rural South.

In this portrait of his niece, Johnson used only six colors: red, yellow, blue, green, brown, and white. He constructed the figure and doll carriage in

expressive but simple forms set against an empty background. He painted a few details—the girl's finger- and toenails and her hair ribbon—in a graphic, almost childlike style. Johnson created a playful image that belies his mastery of color.

Through the use of colors that appear to advance or recede, Johnson created the sensation of depth and space. Using pairs of complementary colors, he created strong contrasts. Johnson mixed clear, bright shades of lavender blue, green, and red that seem closer to us than the yellow background. Through the dark umber skin tone, Johnson depicted the girl in a space defined by color rather than by traditional perspective drawing.

Johnson is one of three prominent African-American painters whose work was featured in the landmark exhibition Harlem Renaissance, organized in 1987 by The Studio Museum in Harlem.

Johnson painted the doll-carriage wheels with expressive lines that convey a feeling of movement.

GIRL ON A BALCONY, 1983
Fernando Botero, Colombian (born 1932), oil on canvas, 48⅛" x 35"

Fernando Botero decided to become an artist when he was a teenager in Colombia. At age twenty-one, Botero moved to Italy to continue his education. There he studied the murals of Andrea Mantegna (1431–1506). In the fifteenth century, Mantegna had solved the most difficult technical problem for painters: he created the illusion of three-dimensional forms and depth on the flat surface of a painting.

Inspired by the majestic presence of Mantegna's larger-than-life-size figures, Botero began to distort the size of the people he depicted. By painting figures that are extremely fat, Botero emphasizes his point of view that the essence of human beauty is found in the rounded forms of well-fed people.

Applying his own standards of beauty to this young girl, Botero depicts her majestic figure and billowing coils of hair. The buttons of her dress, the cherry earrings, and the landscape of balloonlike trees emphasize the overall effect of roundness.

Botero built up the girl's ample form in thin layers of paint on a canvas covered with a salmon pink base coat, or ground. The original layer of pink paint glows through the pale skin tones that he defined with miniaturized details—facial features and hands that are tiny compared to the figure. He painted in cool, toned-down colors with even brushstrokes, creating a smooth finish that suggests porcelain.

Although this figure is greatly distorted, the painting is not satirical or mean. Botero avoids making fun of his subject through his gentle sense of humor and polished technical skill.

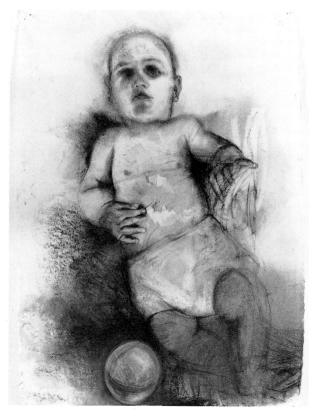

Contemporary artist Jim Dine (born 1935) made a drawing that looks like a painting through the use of charcoal, which he softened and blended with a brush dipped in oil.

Glossary and Index

1. Paint is made by combining finely powdered pigment with a vehicle. A vehicle is a fluid that evenly disperses the color. The kind of vehicle used sometimes gives the paint its name, for example: oil paint. Pigment is the raw material that gives paint its color. Pigments can be made from natural minerals and from artificial chemical compounds.

2. Paint is made thinner or thicker with a substance called a medium, which can produce a consistency like that of water or mayonnaise or peanut butter.

3. A solvent must be used by the painter to clean the paint from brushes, tools, and the hands. The solvent must be appropriate for the composition of the paint.

OIL PAINT: Pigment is combined with an oil vehicle (usually linseed or poppy oil). The medium chosen by most artists is linseed oil. Oil paint is never mixed with water; the solvent is turpentine. Oil paint dries slowly, which enables the artist to work on a painting for a long time. Some painters add other materials, such as pumice powder or marble dust, to produce thick layers of color. Oil paint has been used since the fifteenth century. Until the early nineteenth century, artists or their assistants ground the pigment and combined the ingredients of paint in their studios. When the flexible tin tube (like a toothpaste tube) was invented in 1840, paint made by art suppliers became available.

TEMPERA: Pigment is combined with a water-based vehicle. The paint is combined with raw egg yolk to "temper" it into a mayonnaiselike consistency usable with a brush. The solvent for tempera is water. Tempera was used by the ancient Greeks and was the favorite method of painters in medieval Europe. It is now available in tubes, ready to use. The painter supplies the egg yolk.

WATERCOLOR: Pigment is combined with gum arabic, a water-based vehicle. Water is both the medium and the solvent. Watercolor paint now comes ready to use in tubes (moist) or in cakes (dry). Watercolor paint is thinned with water, and areas of paper are often left uncovered to produce highlights.

Gouache is an opaque form of watercolor, which is also called tempera or body color.

Watercolor paint was first used 37,000 years ago by cave dwellers who created the first wall paintings.

PALETTE, 36: (1) A flat tray used by a painter for laying out and mixing colors. (2) The range of colors selected by a painter for a work.

PATRON, 7, 12, 16: One who supports the arts or an individual artist.

PERSPECTIVE, 34, 42: Perspective is a method of representing people, places, and things in a painting or drawing to make them appear solid or three-dimensional rather than flat. Six basic rules of perspective are used in Western art.

1. People in a painting appear larger when near and gradually become smaller as they get farther away.

2. People in the foreground overlap people or objects behind them.

3. People become closer together as they get farther away.

4. People in the distance are closer to the top of the picture than those in the foreground.

5. Colors are brighter and shadows are stronger in the foreground. Colors and shadows are paler and softer in the background. This technique is often called *atmospheric perspective*.

6. Lines that, in real life, are parallel (such as the line of a ceiling and the line of a floor) are drawn at an angle, and the lines meet at the *horizon line*, which represents the eye level of the artist and the viewer.

In addition, a special technique of perspective, called *foreshortening*, is used to compensate for distortion in figures and objects painted on a flat surface. For example, an artist will paint the hand of an outstretched arm larger than it is in proportion to the arm, which becomes smaller as it recedes toward the shoulder. This correction, necessary in a picture using perspective, is automatically made by the human eye observing a scene in life. *Foreshortening* refers to the representation of figures or objects, whereas *perspective* refers to the representation of a scene or a space.

Painters have used these methods to depict objects in space since the fifteenth century. But many twentieth-century artists choose not to use perspective. An artist might emphasize colors, lines, or shapes to express an idea instead of showing people or objects in a realistic space.

PORTRAIT: A painting, drawing, sculpture, or photograph that represents an individual's appearance and, usually, his or her personality.

SCALE, 32: The relationship of the size of an object to that of a human figure. For example: in a painting that depicts a mountain, we can judge the mountain's size only if we compare it to that of a human figure.

SHADOW, 8, 20, 22, 28, 34: An area made darker than its surroundings because direct light does not reach it.

SKETCH, 36: A quickly made drawing.

TONE, 18, 20, 24, 26: The sensation of an overall coloration in a painting. For example, an artist might begin by painting the entire picture in shades of greenish gray. After more colors are applied using transparent glazes, shadows, and highlights, the mass of greenish gray color underneath will show through and create an even tone, or *tonal harmony*.

One of the ways that painters working with opaque colors can achieve the same effect is by adding one color, such as green, to every other color on their palette. This makes all of the colors seem more alike, or harmonious. The effect of tonal harmony is part of the artist's vision and begins with the first brushstrokes. It cannot be added to a finished painting. *See also* COLOR

TRANSPARENT, 8, 12, 16: Allowing light to pass through so colors underneath can be seen. (The opposite of OPAQUE)

TURPENTINE, 18, 36: A strong-smelling solvent, made from pine sap, used in oil painting. *See also* PAINT: OIL PAINT

Van Dyck, Anthony, 18 (Pronounced Van Dike)
Velázquez, Diego Rodríguez de Silva, 20

Credits